D1325066

Also by Adeline Foo

1 **THE DIARY OF AMOS LEE**
I Sit, I Write, I Flush!

2 **THE DIARY OF AMOS LEE**
Girls, Guts and Glory!

3 **THE DIARY OF AMOS LEE**
I'm Twelve, I'm Tough, I Tweet!

3.5 **THE DIARY OF AMOS LEE**
Your D.I.Y. Toilet Diary to Fame!

4 **THE DIARY OF AMOS LEE**
Lights, Camera, Superstar!

1 **WHOOPIE LEE**
Almost Famous

2 **WHOOPIE LEE**
The Big Spell Off

Find out more at
www.amoslee.com.sg

Visit **www.facebook.com/thewhoopieleediaries**
to stand a chance to win prizes! Click 'Like' and tell
us what you've enjoyed about the book!

Whoopie Lee
THE BiG SPELL OFF

Written by
ADELINE FOO

Illustrated by
STEPHANIE WONG

EPIGRAM BOOKS/SINGAPORE

**PUBLISHED IN SINGAPORE
BY EPIGRAM BOOKS**
www.epigrambooks.sg

Cover design by Stephanie Wong
Illustrations © 2013 Stephanie Wong

**NATIONAL LIBRARY BOARD SINGAPORE
CATALOGUING IN PUBLICATION DATA**
Foo, Adeline, 1971—
Whoopie Lee: The Big Spell Off / Written by Adeline Foo;
Illustrated by Stephanie Wong.—Singapore: Epigram Books, c2013.
p. cm.
ISBN: 978-981-07-4780-0 (pbk.)
ISBN: 978-981-07-4781-7 (ePub)

1. Girls—Singapore—Juvenile fiction. 2. Friendship—Juvenile fiction.
3. Fame—Juvenile fiction. I. Wong, Stephanie, 1979— II. Title.

PZ7
S823—dc23   OCN821793571

Printed in Singapore

10 9 8 7 6 5 4 3 2 1

I'm Whoopie, named after the Big Oreo Pie! I'm the
middle child, the sweet, creamy vanilla frosting stuck
between two boring brothers. I like to think I'm special,
but well… maybe only in my parents' eyes.

My brothers are really the centre of Mum's attention!
I'm always the good one, the one who doesn't get into
trouble, the one who studies and does all her homework
without being nagged at. But that means I don't get much
notice, do I?

At school, I'm not exactly the most popular girl either. Not when your best friend is a big star who gets all the attention, because she has acted in two shows! TWO! One was directed by Oliver Stone (err, who's that?) Anyway, the second one was a local production called *The Pooplitzer Choice*. But even though I acted alongside her, no one remembered ME.

I've even tried to do some really silly things, like train a HUMAN POODLE. That's right, not just any poodle but one that can sing, dance and twirl the hula hoop beautifully. I made my best friend, Morticia, the one that starred in the two shows, act as my poodle. But still, that hasn't made me famous! So I've been thinking really, really HARD. I want to do something to make people notice me.

2 January

I want to be famous!

Morticia
So do I!

Let's do something.

Morticia
Like win something?

Singing contest?

Morticia
Lame.

Dance contest?

Morticia
Naaah.

A feat?

Morticia
That's exactly what ALL Singaporeans think of when they want to be famous. I want to be special!

Think of something then, GENIUS.

Morticia
Win a contest that will make us famous!

Oh okay. The Math Olympiad?

Morticia
Is that a sport?

No, silly. What about the Science Olympiad?

Morticia
It's not a sport? What is it?

I know! I know! The Spelling Championship!

Morticia
Er... wazzat?

I saw it on TV last year! Kids get to spell words. The winner is the last one standing!

Morticia
Let's do it! How do we train?

LEARN ALL THE WORDS in the dictionary!

Morticia
WHAT! There must be an easier way! What about last year's contest? We can learn all the words that appeared!

GENIUS! We must get that list!

Morticia
You go find out.

And you will help me to learn the words?

Morticia
YOU help me to learn the words! I want to be Spelling Bee champ!

But there can only be ONE winner.

Morticia
And it will be ME!

But you are my best friend! And it's my idea!

Morticia
But I don't want to fight with you. Why don't you join next year? You help me first!

Morticia
Hellllllloooo... are you there?

I'm not sure about this.

Morticia
You're doing this for me! Now I must pick my winning dress to wear. Got to go. Bye!

I never expected our conversation to turn out this way.
I couldn't describe the feelings that I went through. Hurt?
Resentment? But I shouldn't be feeling this way! Morticia
is my best friend. I should be thrilled for her, right? I was
really disappointed when I turned off my handphone.

I thought we would both be having fun, training to be the
champions of Singapore's greatest Spell Off! Guess I
was wrong. But maybe I can still persuade her to let me
join. Best friends always look out for each other, right?

It's good to be back at school. I was still a little upset with Morticia, so I refused to take the seat beside her. But by the end of the day, we were back as friends. Thanks to a new English teacher who had taken our class. Of all the names in the world, his mother chose to name him Noah Webster! After the dictionary! We thought he was joking when he told us his mother was crazy about collecting dictionaries. That really got us cracked up. Then someone asked if he was married to Miss Oxford or Miss Cambridge. He just chuckled and said he was pleased we are a clever bunch. Morticia and I really like him! He's sooooo cool!

FACEBOOK

Whoopie Lee
Tuesday

My teacher. A modern-day Einstein with slick back hair.

Like • Comment • Share   80

I love his trousers! I could have sworn they are bell-bottoms. I've seen the same style of trousers hanging in Grandpa's cupboard. Imagine that, a teacher named after the *Webster's Dictionary*.

I told Mr. Webster after class that I'm training with Morticia to enter the Spelling Championship. He was thrilled when he heard that! He offered to train us immediately. This is FANTASTIC! We are sooooo going to need all the help we can get!

I did some research on famous movies and books that were written about Spelling Bee Champions. It was AWESOME to read about these stories. Here's a list:

Whoopie's Spelling Bee Champs' List

1. *The Girl Who Spelled Freedom*
   This story is based on the real life events of Linn Yann, a Cambodian refugee who became a National Spelling Bee finalist in the United States. The story was made into a Disney film!

2. *Spellbound*
   A documentary about eight children in a National Spelling Bee finals. It was even nominated for an Academy Award! (Imagine that, these kids must be so FAMOUS!)

3. *Bee Season*, a movie starring Richard Gere and Juliette Binoche
   The story is about a family on a downward spiral when the father becomes obsessed with training his 11-year-old daughter to become the

spelling bee champion, at the expense of the other family members. (Hmmm... this doesn't sound like a 'happy movie'! But imagine being cast in a movie when you're only 11! That's sooooo cool!)

4. *Akeelah and the Bee*
About Akeelah Anderson, an 11-year-old girl from a poor family who has a gift for words. Despite the objections of her mother, she overcomes school bullies to enter many spelling contests to earn the chance to compete for a spot in the American Scripps National Spelling Bee. (And of course, she wins!)

Isn't this awesome? There are sooooo many inspirations! All these people got famous by getting involved in the Spelling Bee competition! This is going to be an AMAZING EXPERIENCE for me!

I spent my afternoon in the teachers' common room after school. I offered to tidy up the students' art and craft corner so that I can eavesdrop on the conversations! It took me almost two hours before I was done cleaning up several months' worth of recycled junk, dust trappings and other unmentionables, like lizard droppings!

Eeiuwww! But my hard work paid off. I heard one of the English teachers mention that last year's Spelling Championship had words that were taken from a book, *Commonly Misspelt Words*. Another teacher also said that she remembered several words were derived from 'Idioms'. THIS IS GREAT! I can't wait to tell Morticia!

Just before I left the common room, I took a couple of pictures for my Facebook page. See what I made from JUNK that I managed to salvage!

Whoopie Lee
Tuesday

Whoopie's many uses of toilet-paper holders—Dinosaurs alive! Raaarrr!

Pterosaur

Archaeopteryx

Tyrannosaurus Rex

Like · Comment · Share   289

486 people like this.

View all 30 comments

Morticia Phui
Who cares about extint dinosaurs!

But what I didn't expect was to have Morticia post a rude comment on my Facebook.

I was FURIOUS! I called her up immediately. She said I was wasting my time fiddling with 'disgusting junk'. I was so MAD I almost screamed at her! I told her it was my strategy to get my hands on last year's list of words that was used in the Spelling Championship! Sometimes I wonder why she's my best friend. She didn't say anything. But I got in the last word. I told her she misspelt 'e-x-t-i-n-c-t'. Seriously, she has to work really hard if she wants to be Spelling Bee Champion. Humph.

Whoopie's List of Commonly Misspelt Words

-A-	-B-	-C-
absence	baffle	calendar
advice (noun)	beginning	camouflage
advise (verb)	believe	chief
accidentally	breath	commemorate
accommodate	breathe	congratulations
accumulate	broccoli	criticise
achieve	buffet	crooked
acquire	bulge	crossover
affix	buoy	crutch
agitation	burly	cuckoo
airborne	burrow	culinary
allergy	buttress	cutlery

Mr. Webster passed Morticia and me a couple of exercises to help us with learning new words. It was sooooo fun that I forgot I was mad with Morticia. Anyway, she apologised for being rude. She even gave me a cute dinosaur button for my new notebook. Guess we're cool now.

Mr. Webster's Spell-Aloud Tips

- Keep a notebook. Fill it with words copied from newspapers, magazines, brochures, food menus and anything else you can get your hands on!
- Grab a friend to test you on a word picked from the above list.
- Spell the word three times. Do you know its meaning? If you don't, check the *Webster's Dictionary*!
- Prepare a list of the words you misspelt. Tape it to your pencil case. Learn these words every time you reach for a pencil or pen.
- Exchange your notebook with a friend. Learn the words on your friend's list! This will immediately double the number of words you know!

Mum was really pleased with my newfound interest in learning to spell new words. She said I've never given her reason to worry, unlike my brothers. Is that some kind of compliment?

Poor Mum. These days, she's so busy with driving Everest around for all his enrichment classes. That, after attending full-day kindergarten! Let's see, Mondays and Wednesdays, he has swimming class. Tuesdays and Thursdays, it's taekwondo. Fridays, Saturdays and Sundays, it's abacus training and reading. My little brother is so busy, I have to make an appointment when I want to play with him! He's so pitiful—totally exhausted after all his classes! When I see him at 8pm after I've done my homework, he's usually fast asleep! I asked Mum why she's making Everest go through so many classes; she didn't have a good answer. She said she was only trying to keep up with the other Mums who are driven to make sure their children know everything before they enrol in primary school. Didn't these women hear what the Prime Minister said? I remember jumping for joy when I heard him say on TV, "No homework is not a bad thing!" And he DISTINCTLY said, "Let our children PLAY more!"

Just before bedtime, Mum told me she was "totally 100%" behind my spelling training. Hmmm… this doesn't sound good. I wonder what she's up to.

Mr. Webster spoke to Morticia and me about taking our Spelling Bee training more seriously. He wanted me to work on a list of words derived from topics he had identified. He must have sensed Morticia's reluctance because he said sharply to her, "If you want to win, you have to work hard! There's no shortcut!" I poked her hard in the ribs when I saw her stifling a yawn. Seriously, what is her problem?

I nodded eagerly to Mr. Webster and promised him that I would be diligent. He gave me a handwritten note when he left the classroom:

Words from Life Sciences derived from the Triassic, Jurassic and Cretaceous periods

What, like dinosaurs? I have two brothers, I know all about dinosaurs!

Words commonly used in Idioms

Haha! I knew it! This was what I heard in the teachers' common room too!

Words inspired by trends and pop culture, etc.

Wow. This is a lot of work! I asked Morticia if we could split up the task. I was hurt when she snorted rudely and said she was going with her mother to have her hair done.

Huh? We're only 10! What's there to do with our hair? After some bugging, she admitted that she's not really interested in doing the research. I was really disappointed with her confession! I thought we were in it together!

Amos peed in his pants from laughing too hard when I said I was training Morticia to be the Spelling Bee champ. He ran into the toilet and even made a big show of changing his trousers!

What is it with him? I can't understand why he dislikes Morticia so much! He was really mean when he said, "That DODO? They should just get her to ring the bell when kids misspell a word! DIIIINNNGGG! You're OUT!"

He was such an annoying busybody that when I wasn't looking, he added a few hastily-written idioms in my research notes. They're quite funny, but I shouldn't be laughing as she's my best friend.

Morticia, the Spelling Bee Wannabe

Dear Sis, your task is <u>as dead as a dodo</u>.
It's hopeless with no chance
of success! Morticia is <u>dull</u>
<u>as dishwater</u>. She's totally
uninspiring and uninteresting!

You are <u>casting pearls before</u>
<u>swine</u>. That means doing
something good on someone
who doesn't appreciate it, silly!

Ever heard of this? You are <u>flogging a dead horse</u>.
This is like pursuing a useless goal! Please, get real.
Stop fantasising!

amos lee

Who would have thought that he can write so well!

MY THOUGHTS ABOUT MORTICIA

We have been friends since we were in Primary One.
That's like THREE years! We have always done everything
together! We used to listen to music together and learn
how to sing and dance.

We have even auditioned to act in shows. I've also written a play casting her as a lead actor!

But I know we are both very different. For one, she doesn't like to study. I find that odd as her brother, Michael, was a former top student in our school! But Morticia is fun to hang out with. She can be really silly and funny, and I do adore her company. We love drawing and painting, and chatting on WhatsApp. I can't imagine not talking to her for a single day.

I'm still hurt that she has asked me NOT to participate in the Spelling Championship. Last night while I was in bed, I found myself suddenly wishing that she would develop a bad cough. Anything, to stop her from taking part in the Spell Off!

Then guess what happened? This morning when I woke up, I found myself COUGHING without a reason! I recalled my BAD WISH on Morticia, and suddenly it hit me that because I was so MEAN and EVIL… the bad thing happened to ME!

Oh my goodness! What have I done? I had to drink lots and lots of water before I felt better. Guess I shouldn't wish bad things on someone else. I know Morticia will need all the help she can get. That's what I must do. Help her study the words because she's my best friend.

I didn't expect Mum to champion word-learning and correct bad spelling! I saw a series of posts she made on Facebook! She also tagged me, Amos, Morticia and ALL OUR CLASSMATES to view them! So this is her way of supporting me in learning to spell right!

That post went viral! Mum received hundreds of likes within one hour! Hey… It's cool having a Mum who's a Bad-English Buster! I can learn a thing or two.

I saw Morticia's Facebook post. I couldn't believe she even had her dress for the Championship picked out! What's with the headdress? She looks like a stupid BIRD! Like a real DODO for crying out loud!

Isn't this like counting your chickens before they are hatched? How does she know she's going to win the Spelling Championship?

I left a message on her wall.

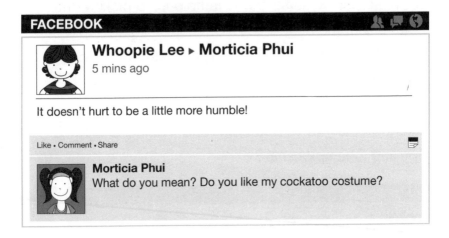

So she knows she looks like one. This is so incredible.

During Math class, Morticia asked what was taking me so long to compile the list of words used in last year's Spelling Championship. I ignored her and focused on doing my sums. I was sooooo mad! I'm doing all the hard work and all she does is nag me! I looked across at her. She seemed pleased with doodling something in her notebook. I stretched my head as close as I could to see what she was doing. Imagine my surprise when I saw her doing sketches of BIRDS! It was Math class, for goodness sake!

Then, suddenly, something strange came over me.
I felt my hand shoot up and wave madly to the teacher.
An alien voice came out from my mouth, and I heard it
saying, "Morticia is drawing BIRDS in her notebook!"

I was horrified with myself! I looked at Morticia just as her
head shot up! She looked at me, caught by surprise. I saw
her looking stricken and betrayed and I felt really GUILTY!
I almost cried out in alarm when I saw the teacher striding
over to her desk. I thought he would be mad, but instead,
he picked up her notebook, studied her drawings and…
looked amused! Then he told her to put it away. I couldn't
believe it when he patted her on the head and actually
said, "Do the school proud. I heard from Mr. Webster that
you're participating in the Spelling Championship!"

My jaw dropped wide open. Morticia then turned to
look at me. She gave me a thumbs-up and grinned in
triumph. I must have looked like a JEALOUS PARROT!
I slammed my mouth shut and looked down at my table.
I felt really rotten for having told on my best friend.
What is happening to me?

After school, I was surprised when Morticia passed
me a present. It was a dress, same as the one she had
posted on her Facebook. It was really pretty! It's white with
ruffles! I choked back on my tears. She had done this for

me when I had almost got her into trouble? I am such a HORRIBLE friend!

Morticia said excitedly, "My mother made it for us! Do you like it? We are SOOOOO going to be FAMOUS!" I smiled a little and hugged the dress. Although I didn't like the idea of looking like a cockatoo, I thought it was really sweet of her. I thanked her and we hugged. She didn't even ask why I squealed on her.

Back to the grind. This is it. I am determined to help Morticia train to be the BEST Spelling Bee champ, EVER!

Whoopie's List of Commonly Misspelt Words

-D-	-E-	-F-
definitely	easily	familiar
desperate	embarrass	festival
develop	exaggerate	fiery
difference	exercise	finally
disappear	existence	forty
disappoint	experience	furniture

I told Morticia that she had to study all the words that I was compiling. That would be hundreds of words that are commonly misspelt! And another list to be compiled from Mr. Webster's suggestions; those derived from the origins of dinosaurs, idioms, trends and pop culture.

I tried asking her again if maybe she would let us both compete. But she looked so scared and unsure. Then she said that it would totally destroy our friendship! Although I was disappointed, I believed her.

Morticia promised that she would do her best to memorise all the words. That comforted me. At least my efforts would not be wasted!

Mum is getting quite a following on Facebook. She had posted a picture of a noodle stall taken at a hawker centre.

WEEK 06

There's no Shortcut

After school, Morticia came over to my flat. I was puzzled when she started talking about developing some form of hand signal for the Spelling Championship. "Whatever for?" I asked.

"Well... there might be words that I can't spell. You can help me by signing the letters from the audience!"

I was SHOCKED! How could she even think of that! That's CHEATING! I was so indignant that I yelled at her! "Maybe if you forget about what to wear and how famous you're going to be, you might find the time to memorise the words I'm compiling!" That DIVA! She had the cheek to look hurt. I was suspicious when she started sniffling and dabbing a handkerchief at her eyes. "How could you say that? So you won't help your best friend?"

"This is SERIOUS! If we get caught, we could be expelled! I would be a total disgrace to my family! My mother would KILL me!" I wailed. But before I could say anything else, she turned her back on me and said coolly, "Calm down. You're over-reacting."

What? I'm over-reacting? Seriously? I don't believe this! What's next? She might as well suggest that I write out the word on a white sheet and prompt her from the audience! Hand signals? What a ridiculous idea!

WEEK
07

THiNKiNG OUT OF the BOX

I thought of a really clever plan to make Morticia start studying. When I had to babysit Everest and he was naughty, I used to surf the Internet for scary pictures to frighten him into obeying me. It worked every time. I found a really awesome picture and had it printed in several copies on sticker paper. After school, I went to Morticia's flat and her mother let me in without asking any questions.

I found four spots for sticking my pictures. In her bedroom, on two wall mirrors, on the toilet mirror, and in the last hiding spot, her desk drawer, where I know she keeps a silver Barbie mirror. I left the flat gloating, happy at having accomplished my task.

Then I waited for her call. It came exactly at nine o'clock. Her last check in the mirror before going to bed. Just as I had expected, she was wailing pitifully, "Okay, okay! You win! I'm going to study the stupid spelling list NOW!" I doubled over from laughing hysterically! It was sooooo funny!

Stop looking in the mirror. You should be studying!

Here's the picture I stuck on all of Morticia's mirrors. There's no way she wouldn't get my message.

OH NO! Amos saw the picture of the ugly condor I saved on Mum's laptop! The IDIOT! He posted the picture on Facebook with a caption! How could he! Morticia's going to KILL me!

The Spelling Bee Condor post went viral! Hmmm… maybe the prank wasn't such a bad thing. Morticia wasn't mad at what Amos did. In fact, she was rather pleased with all the attention she got! Last I checked, she said she had learnt all the words I had given her; she even said she was waiting for more! Maybe my brother is a genius after all.

Facebook Posts by Mum, the Bad-English Buster

Around the period between 225 and 65 million years ago, dinosaurs were once dominant land animals.

This was a time when many species evolved and became extinct. It is hard to believe that dinosaurs like the giant predator Tyrannosaurus Rex and the smallest hummingbird once shared a common heritage. Palaeontologists divide dinosaurs into two distinct lineages: the bird-hipped ornithischians and the lizard-hipped saurischians. The bird-hipped plant-eating dinosaurs include the ornithopods (duck-billed dinosaurs) and the dome-headed (pachycephalosaurid), horned (ceratopsians: rhinoceros-like) and armoured (stegosaur) dinosaurs.

The lizard-hipped saurischians were closer to the pterosaurs, their first cousins, and to birds, their descendants. Saurischians include the long-necked dinosaurs, like the Apatosaurus, the Brachiosaurus and the Diplodocus, and also all meat-eating dinosaurs, the theropods.

Most theropods had lizard-like hips, but some, like the Velociraptor, had hips that were similar to those of primitive birds like the Archaeopteryx.

ABOUT THE THEROPODS

They had the same basic body shape and they were bipedal like modern birds and humans. Their arms were always shorter than their hind legs, like the Tyrannosaurus. Theropods could be tiny or they could be huge. Some familiar ones that would come to mind are the T. rex, the Oviraptor and the large-brained birdlike Troodon. Birds evolved from theropods before the end of the Jurassic period. This would be about 150 million years ago. But many of the more birdlike theropod specimens date from the Late Cretaceous, some 50 to 85 million years later.

The Late Cretaceous birdlike dinosaurs provide a hint of the evolutionary transition from dinosaurs to birds and they also tell us how closely birds and theropods were once related.

So, really, who would have guessed that the T. rex, the dodo and the condor would be described as being related to one another!

I spent two ENTIRE days reading from so many books on dinosaurs before I could complete my article. And guess what Morticia had to say?

"It's too difficult to remember all the names! I hate these STUPID BIRD-BRAINED GIANTS! Forget this list of words!" Seriously, if any of these words appear at the Spelling Championship, I'm going to see who's the real bird brain.

Whoopie's List of Commonly Misspelt Words

-G-	-H-	-I-
garbage	handkerchief	imaginary
giraffe	harass	immediately
gorgeous	height	incredible
grammar	hiccup	independent
guarantee	holiday	interruption
gutsy	humorous	irrelevant
gutter	hunch	irremovable
guttural	hurtle	irreparable
guzzle	hustle	irresponsible
gymnasium	hygiene	issue

More Facebook Posts by Mum

TheRealTigerMum
Tuesday

Emergency Exit. <u>Open</u> this door will trigger the security alarm! (Change it to "Opening"!)

Caution! <u>Slippy</u> road (Slippery!)

and the grossest:

SPECIAL BREW PASSED BY MASTER CHEF!

Like • Comment • Share   150

262 people like this.

View all 80 comments

TheRealTigerMum
Maybe they mean, "Recipe for brew is developed by Master Chef?"

Seriously, someone should pay my mother for going around Singapore correcting English on signages!

Oh my goodness! There was a HUGE registration exercise to get students to sign up for the Spelling Championship!

This morning during assembly, a deejay team from a local radio station made their way to our school to conduct a Spelling Bee game. Everyone was so thrilled, the excitement, the tension... Oh my goodness, some students even cried when they were knocked out! Oh pleeeaaasee... it's only a demonstration of the Spelling Championship event! But I was sooooo happy when I got to go on stage to play the game. The word I received was 'achieve'. I knew that one for sure! It was on my list of commonly misspelt words! I got it right and guess what I got for a prize? A really cute mouse pad! It was awesome! It even had a caption: "All Abuzz with the Spelling Bee!"

After the trial, the Principal announced that students who were selected would go on to participate in the Spelling Championship preliminaries, zonals and finals. The Spelling Bee Champion will take home $5,000 in cash! Wow, that's a lot of money! And there was a bigger surprise waiting after the Principal's announcement.

Mr. Webster said that he had decided to pick me to be interviewed by a newspaper reporter! Who, ME? YES! I was over the moon! I couldn't believe I was going to appear in the newspapers! I had to tell Morticia immediately!

Have you heard?

Morticia
Yes, yes, yes! Isn't it exciting?

Is it okay if I wear the new dress?

Morticia
No! Save it for the Championship!

But I have nothing to wear!

Morticia
Why do you care? You have nothing to do with the contest!

Morticia
Hellllloooooo?

But Mr. Webster said I would be speaking to the reporter!?

Morticia
I told him the reporter can speak to me.

WHAT?!

Morticia
You get your turn next year! I'm going first. We agreed! Remember?

But I know all the words! I've been working hard to compile the spelling list! I really want to sign up for the Spelling Championship!

Morticia
You can sign up next year!

Morticia
Hellllloooooo?

Morticia
Hey, you there?

Morticia
You reading this?

Morticia
Yoohooo!!!!!

The silent treatment kills. I'm SOOOOO UPSET with her! How can she do this to me! Mr. Webster picked ME! I was going to be interviewed by the reporter! And now everything is falling apart! Oooohh how I hate her!

I was so angry with Morticia that I didn't tell her I was signing up for the Championship. I'm doing it just to SPITE her! I don't care if we DESTROY our FRIENDSHIP! I was so fired up that I stayed back after school to do more research. Mr. Webster saw me at the library. He asked why Morticia wasn't with me. I lied that she had something else to do and had gone home. He must have guessed that I was lying. He patted me on the head and said gently, "It's only a contest. Don't lose your best friend because of this."

How did he guess? I felt really bad after what he said. I went home immediately and called Morticia. She sounded really relieved to hear from me. "I'm sooooo sorry I was so selfish!" I swallowed the lump in my throat. The lie weighed heavily on me. I almost blurted out that I had registered for the Championship. Then she said, "I'll share my prize money with you! I promise, okay? Just let me win it this year. You won't sign up, will you?"

My hurt turned into something else. Resentment? What is wrong with her? Why can't both of us sign up together? What is she afraid of? I've helped her with compiling the word list; I wasn't going to stop till I've finished what Mr. Webster set me out to do! But after a long pause, I gave in. The tension was KILLING ME! I said in a small voice. "Forget it. If you win, I don't want your money. I'm your best friend, I'll help you." Morticia was so pleased

that she screamed loudly on the other end of the phone.
I thought my eardrum was going to burst!

That night, I sent Mr. Webster an email. I told him that
I was withdrawing from the contest as I've promised
Morticia that I would focus on helping her instead.
He replied immediately. "Glad to see that both of you
have made up. Remember, it doesn't matter who wins
this Championship, you're BOTH doing this for the
experience and fun!" I CRIED when I read that line!
But does Morticia know how badly I want to participate?
It was MY IDEA in the first place! And she's supposed
to be my BEST FRIEND! Why is she doing this to me?

Whoopie's List of Commonly Misspelt Words

- J -	- K -	- L -
jackal	kennel	laboratory
jammed	kernel	lavender
jangle	ketchup	length
January	khaki	library
jealousy	kindergarten	likelihood
judgement	knowledge	lying
juvenile	knuckle	luxury

Close to 1,200 primary school students took part in the first round of contest. Morticia was one of them. I felt really small when I was waiting for her outside the test venue. I thought people were giving me weird looks! Like, why wasn't I in there with the rest? Am I not good enough?

After one hour, the written test was over. Morticia was really excited when she saw me. She hugged me hard and said my list of words really helped! She thought she did okay.

I was eagerly waiting to hear about the words that were tested. They were all easy! I could have spelt them too! 'Natural', 'fuchsia', 'diphtheria' and 'menagerie'… I know all of them!

I had to force myself to put aside my jealousy. I wanted sooooo badly to be in the room! I had mixed feelings when Morticia used all of her pocket money to buy me an ice cream. She only had enough for one cone. I offered to share it with her, but she said no. "You have it. I couldn't have done this test without you!"

I ate the ice cream silently. I didn't feel like I deserved it. I wanted to HIT her in the face with it! I could have been in the room if she hadn't forced me NOT to participate! But I was afraid when the BAD THOUGHT popped into my head. And just as I had expected, something bad happened: I dropped the ice cream when I went up the school bus. I stepped on it and lost my footing! Good thing Morticia was standing right behind me. She caught me just in time. Pheeeeew! I would have been splattered with ice cream if she had been slow. But I didn't expect her to be upset. She was going on and on about the money she could have saved. What was she talking about?

That night, I told myself again that I must stop wishing bad things on Morticia. It's just not something a best friend would do.

Results were out: 108 students made it through the test.
Morticia was one of them. I saw it on her Facebook post.
I was sooooo jealous! And I hate myself for feeling this way!

Shouldn't she be a little more humble?
For goodness sake, this is only Round One!

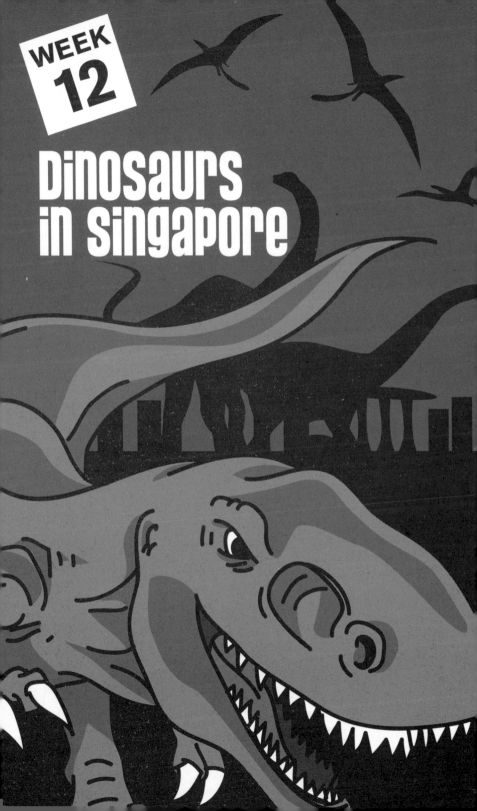

WEEK 12

Dinosaurs in Singapore

Mr. Webster told us about an exciting development today. Imagine, we're getting our very own dinosaurs from the Jurassic times! Ooohh, I can't wait! I wonder what kind of fossils would be exhibited! See, I'm getting really good at spelling. I've learnt to 'see' the word before I spell it: f-o-s-s-i-l. I checked the dictionary: the word refers to "remains of animal or plant life from a geological age". Like dinosaur skeletal remains! AWESOME! I can't wait to tell Morticia!

Here's an article from the newspaper that Mr. Webster circulated!

2014:
Singapore gets its first natural history museum with three giant Diplodocid Sauropod dinosaurs from the Jurassic period!

Museum will house 800,000 Southeast Asian specimens including near-complete fossils of three giant dinosaurs. The largest is 27 metres long!

FROM DINOSAURS TO COCKATOOS

After school, Morticia had a harebrained (or maybe it's bird-brained?) idea for me. She actually suggested that we create a cockatoo dance to perform at the Championship! Eeeiuw… What a stupid idea. My face must have shown dismay. She screeched angrily in response, "You think I won't win? It's going to be my victory dance!"

I really don't know what to say. She's taking this fantasy way too seriously! She has only learned half of what I've prepared for the spelling training… and she thinks she's going to win?

But because I'm her best friend, I got sucked into doing the dance. She can be really persuasive when she wants to. I didn't expect it to be so addictive. She had this cute snazzy jingle recorded on her phone to go with the dance. Before long, we were dancing, flapping our wings and shaking our butts over and over again till more and more kids joined us!

When I was ready to go home, I was surprised when I realised that we had been practising for TWO HOURS! Really, who would have thought? And the number of schoolmates dancing and laughing along with us? About 30 kids!

That's Morticia. She's so funny and silly that people like hanging around her. I forgot I was upset with her. At least for the afternoon. I do like her cockatoo dance. It's cute! Here are the steps.

HOW TO DO THE COCKATOO DANCE!

1 Hold your hands in the position of 'beaks'. Open and close your fingers like a cockatoo's beak.

2 Place your arms like a pair of flapping wings. Flap your wings!

3 Now 'wiggle' your bum like a tuft of feathers! Shake it up and down!

4 Clap your hands!

Repeat everything and IGNORE all the people laughing. Just pretend to be a COCKATOO for the day!

That night, I sent Morticia a message. I texted, "Archaeopteryx, the ancestor of all birds. Learn to spell it!" Her reply came back immediately, "I would learn it just for you. I really hate dinosaur words!"

Mum's Facebook Posts

FACEBOOK

TheRealTigerMum
Wednesday

Sorry, <u>please self-service</u>
(Just use "Self-service" or "Please help yourself"!)

Out of <u>Bounce</u> to Students
(Are they referring to balls that cannot bounce?
It should be "Out of bounds"!)

<u>Thank Queue</u>
(Thank you, please join the queue.)

Like • Comment • Share   5

👍 158 people like this.

💬 View all 15 comments

Anthony
LOL! Wait till you see what my mum found too.

During recess, Morticia was acting strange. She refused to eat anything. I asked if she wasn't feeling well, she said she was saving money. "For what?" I asked. She didn't reply. But I saw her put away two dollars when she thought I wasn't looking. She had the money zipped up carefully in a pouch. When she said she was running to the toilet, I took a peep in the pouch. I was surprised to see several rolled-up dollar notes! I thought guiltily, "This is wrong! I shouldn't be snooping!" Since when had she turned so thrifty? I wonder what she's saving for.

Today was a trial run for the students representing our school in the Spelling Championship. I was excited just like everyone else! I was thrilled that Morticia would be put to a test! A small part of me was hoping to see her blunder… but I pinched myself hard, "NO BAD THOUGHTS!" I whispered fiercely to myself.

The kids around me looked surprised to see me muttering under my breath. I hissed at them when they sniggered. When Morticia came up to me to take my hand, I was surprised that it was clammy. I looked at her with mixed feelings. Was it guilt from looking into her money pouch earlier in the morning, or was it something else, like jealousy?

I brushed my negative feelings aside. I put on a big fake smile and squeezed her hand hard. "Do your best, you can do this!" I nodded encouragingly.

Morticia smiled weakly and ran up stage to take her seat. A teacher walked up to seize the microphone. She spoke into it, loud and clear, "HELLO and welcome to supporting our National Spelling CHAMPIONS!" The cheers and applause that followed were so loud and hearty that I felt sick! I couldn't believe she actually said that!

One by one, the participants on stage were tested on their knowledge of words. I was seated in one of the middle rows in the assembly hall. Mr. Webster had prepared me well with his word categories—idioms, trends, pop culture—so I could take anything! With every word that was given, I carefully wrote each one into my notebook.

'Sustainability', 'stewardship', 'ecosystem', 'conservation' —I knew them all! And there were words associated with digital life, like 'cloud-computing', 'bandwidth' and 'digerati'! I didn't know what some of these words meant, but I could spell them just from listening hard to the way they were pronounced. 'Pachyderm', 'proclivity'… the list went on. I had to say each word out loud to myself every time. I even had to spell every letter slowly just to 'hear' how it sounded. But I was really proud when I got every

word CORRECT! How did I know? Every time I spelt
the word out loud, I waited for the 'Misspelt Bell' to ring,
but it didn't! A ring would mean that the participant is out.
After every time I spelt one word, Morticia would get her
turn. And, amazingly, she got EVERY WORD CORRECT!

When the session ended, I waited eagerly for Morticia to leave the assembly hall. When she appeared, I thought she looked rather pale and nervous, but I brushed the thought aside. I gushed excitedly, "WOW you got every word RIGHT! And guess what? SO DID I!" I showed her my written list of words. She didn't even glance at it. All she did was clutch me hard and breathed urgently into my ear. "Thank goodness you SPELT everything out slowly! I was SO RELIEVED I could read your lips!"

WHAT?! I looked at her in horror! What was she talking about? I was spelling out the letters to MYSELF!

Morticia giggled uncontrollably before continuing, "Can you do this again? I'm sooooo going to be crowned Spelling Bee Champ!" As if that wasn't enough, she had to rub it in by adding, "Have a dictionary with you. Just in case you don't know some of the words!"

I stared at her, my mouth wide open! I was SO SHOCKED that I was SPEECHLESS! I couldn't believe that I had unwittingly been her cheating accomplice! Oh my goodness, what have I done?

I saw from Morticia's Facebook post that she was really serious in studying for the Spelling Championship! I was pleased as she'd found new words that I wasn't even aware of! Hmmm... she must be really motivated by the idea of winning the prize money.

Morticia's Facebook Post

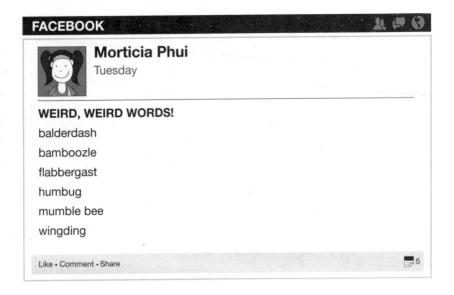

I went over to Morticia's flat after school. WOW! I was SOOOOO SURPRISED to see Post-its plastered all over her flat! And every Post-it contained words she had written, copied from stuff around the house. In the kitchen, I saw words taken from food packagings in the refrigerator and from canned products and bottled sauces in her mother's cupboard:

chilli paste, coriander, cornflour, cumin, galangal, kaffir lime, lemongrass, tamarind, tumeric powder, wasabi

When I used her toilet, I saw Post-its on her bottles of shampoo and bath shower gels, all scribbled with more words! I peeked into the cabinet under the sink, and I saw EVEN MORE words on the Post-its that were pasted on her mother's jars of medicines and ointments.

Who would have thought that she would find a creative way to learn new words! I'm really impressed.

That night, I resolved to work harder to compile more words for training. I stopped myself from thinking BAD THOUGHTS when I secretly wished that Morticia would fall sick or break her leg. I felt really guilty. It was horribly mean to wish those things on your best friend.

WEEK **15**

Training gets Tough

During the week, I didn't stop looking for words. I had completed the list of words that Mr. Webster had assigned, so I asked for more topics to source for new words.

Mr. Webster suggested learning words from 'onomatopoeia'. I looked it up in the dictionary: it meant words that originated as an imitation of natural sounds. People have called it the 'bow-wow' theory: words like 'woof', 'sizzle', 'boink', 'belch', 'clink', 'hiccup', 'squelch', 'vroom' and 'whoop'! This is AWESOME!

I even learnt that some species of birds were named onomatopoeically after the sounds that they make while 'talking'. And one of these birds is Morticia's favourite cockatoo!

BIRDIES THAT TALK:

bobwhite	motmot	willet
curlew	siskin	cuckoo
dickcissel	towhee	cockatoo
kiwi	whippoorwill	

From birds, I moved on to words like names of animals that were derived from the Malay language! It was so COOL to learn these things!

ANIMAL NAMES FROM THE MALAY LANGUAGE, USED BY NATIVES IN SINGAPORE, MALAYSIA, BRUNEI AND BORNEO:

teledu	siamang	lory
cobego	beruang	musang
cassowary	gourami	simpai
pangolin	linsang	tokay

After all the hard work, I couldn't help wishing fervently that I would be given a chance to participate in Singapore's Biggest Spell Off! But a promise is a promise. I told Morticia I would help her, and being the good friend that I am, I emailed her the new list of words that I had compiled.

Message	
FROM:	morticiaphui@yahoo.com
	Dear W, You're the BEST of the best! I'm so thankful that you're my BFF! – Love, M

Aaaawww… I felt all warm and fuzzy when I read her email. That's Morticia, she really knows how to make me feel special. "NO BAD THOUGHTS!" I told myself quickly when I started fantasising about what I could get her to eat that would give her a tummy upset on the day of the contest.

Whoopie's List of Commonly Misspelt Words

-M-	-O-	-Q-
macaroni	obedient	quantity
marshmallow	occasion	quarrel
miniature	occurrence	query
mischievous	official	quiet
misspell	opposite	quite
mysterious	ordinary	quitter
mythical	oriental	quotation
mythology	outrage	quotient

-N-	-P-	-R-
naïve	parallel	receive
necessary	peculiar	recommend
neither	perceive	repetition
netizen	possess	restaurant
niece	probably	rhythm
noticeable	procrastinate	ridiculous
notorious	proficient	rifle
nuisance	prolific	rinse
nuzzle	pronunciation	rivalry

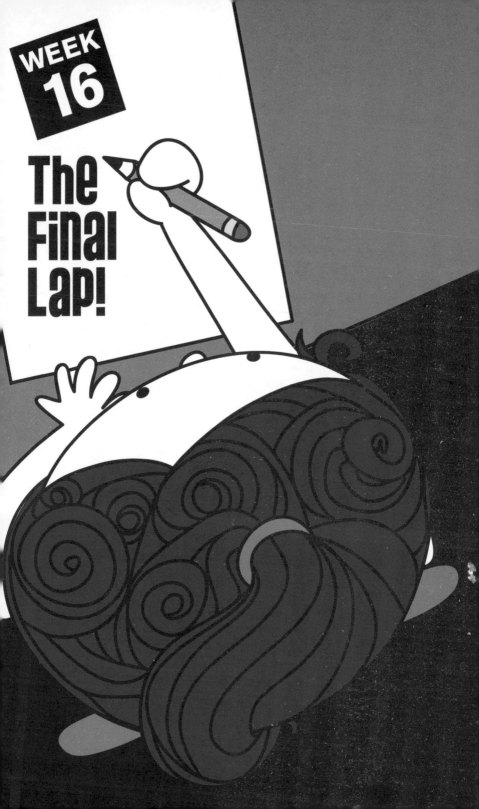

It's two more weeks to the Spelling Championship.
The entire school is all geared up for preparation!

During English class, Mr. Webster tested us on words that
he had compiled. Every time I got a word correct, I would
grin triumphantly to myself. And if I did look up, I would
catch Mr. Webster giving me a thumbs-up. I tried not to
glance at Morticia. She was really nervous, biting her
lower lip and desperately rubbing her hands on her lap.

One time, I even caught her leaning across the aisle
towards the boy beside her to see how he had spelt
a difficult word. When I saw Mr. Webster turning in her
direction, I threw an eraser at the back of her head to
warn her. She glared at me furiously and mouthed an
urgent, "SPELL IT FOR ME!" I looked away and tried hard
not to laugh. It was really fun to tease her. I pretended
I couldn't read her lips. And of course I can't, I'm not a
GENIUS! To think that during the spelling trial, she could
actually read MY LIPS from all the way upstage! That was
an incredible show of her eye power; either that, or she
was really desperate!

After school, Mr. Webster handed me a list of topics to
gather more words for training. I nodded eagerly and
thanked him. When he asked me how Morticia was doing,
I just shrugged. When I saw her run up to catch me, I hid

quickly in the toilet. I couldn't face her after what I did in the classroom. I knew she would be upset. When the coast was clear, I dashed home. Back to learning more words!

Here's a picture of my well-thumbed dictionary, with its many dog-eared pages filled with notes and Post-its:

From Shakespeare, a bearded man who lived a long, long time ago and a famous English playwright whose plays are being studied all over the world, we inherited close to 1,700 popular words and phrases. He created these by playing on words and sounds, focusing on feelings that were derived from the meaning of words. He also tried playing on words by turning nouns and adjectives into verbs, and creating altered forms from the root words.

It would have been impossible to learn all 1,700 words, but here's a list to start with. I found it really exciting to know this bit of history.

addiction, bedazzled, bandit, circumstantial, epileptic, flawed, frugal, hobnob, mimic, moonbeam, quarrelsome, worthless, zany!

Looks like Morticia is back to her pompous, pretentious and grandiloquent ways! I saw a YouTube clip she recorded of herself doing her Cockatoo Dance. And the cheek of it… she actually added a caption that read:

YOUTUBE

0:00/3:25

Better than Gangnam Style! Morticia's Cockatoo Dance! The victory dance of Singapore's Spelling Bee Champ!

Morticia • 38 videos

Subscribe 68

287

220   67

Seriously, I didn't think that the Korean guy who created his rollicking funny horse-riding clip on YouTube would care to compete with a COCKATOO? Someone should teach her not to be boastful. Obviously, she hasn't learnt that pride goes before a fall.

During recess, I was surprised to see Morticia's mother waiting for her. She had with her a box of fried rice she had cooked. Morticia looked really happy to see her mother. I was a little jealous. Mum would never have the time to bring me a packed lunch. She's too busy looking after Everest and posting pictures of Bad English on her Facebook.

I sat beside Morticia while she ate her food. I peered over at her mother. For some reason, my eyes were drawn to her hands. They were gnarled and very rough. My gaze travelled up her arms, they were skinny and taut with protruding veins. She caught me looking and reached over to brush a strand of hair away from my forehead.

I smiled shyly at her. Her face looked so worn out. I remembered Morticia telling me that they were not well-off. Her mother works at a coffeeshop during the day. She is a hawker's assistant, serving cooked food and washing dirty dishes. In the night, she would take on clothes from neighbours in their block, to do alterations for extra money.

I knew that Michael, Morticia's brother, even had to work after school. He helps one of their relatives at a bakery to deliver loaves of freshly baked bread. I turned to my bowl of noodles. I was ashamed to see that it was half eaten.

I didn't like the taste of the soup. I was going to discard it and buy a fresh plate of roti prata. But I didn't.
I forced myself to finish the entire bowl of noodles.

When her Mum left, I saw Morticia quickly putting a two-dollar note in her money pouch. I thought guiltily to myself, "Maybe I shouldn't pick on her so much. She's my best friend, and she's not as well-off as I am."

Whoopie's List of Commonly Misspelt Words

-S-	-U-	-W-
scissors	umbrella	waste
separate	uncomfortable	weather
similar	unconscious	weird
succeed	until	whether
surprise	usually	writing
swagger	utensils	writhe
swollen	utilise	
		-X-
-T-	-V-	xerox
tabulate	vacuum	xylophone
tactics	valuable	
talkative	vanilla	-Y-
taut	vanishing	yacht
temperature	vegetable	yesterday
thorough	veiled	you're
through	villain	
twelfth	visibly	-Z-
twinge	vivacious	zeal
typical	voracious	zodiac

After weeks and weeks of preparation and mugging, FINALLY, the BIG DAY of the Spelling Championship!

We had to make our way to the Suntec City Convention Centre ballroom after school. Participants had to put on their uniforms. But nobody said anything about what supporters had to wear! I wanted to don the new dress that Morticia's Mum had sewn but didn't dare to do so. I tucked the cockatoo headdress into my pocket because something told me that I might need it.

When I spotted Morticia at the venue, I saw that she was a bundle of nerves! She was so anxious that she was stuttering when she spoke to me. "Y-y-you're going to h-help me, right?" she pleaded. I pretended I didn't understand what she meant. Then I looked at her, and BAD THOUGHTS started popping into my head again. "Is she going to be sick, or will she quit because she has decided that I should participate instead? Or maybe I can lock her up in the toilet!" But then the picture of her mother's weary face came into my head. Instead, I heard myself saying, "Do your best. You are going to make your mother proud!" To my surprise, she started crying. And before I could react, her tears turned to loud sobs! I looked around in alarm. I was hoping no one would see or hear us. No such luck. Boys filing into the ballroom started sniggering and nudging one another.

I could hear fierce whispers of "She's scared!" and "Nervous!" going around. A protective instinct rose in me. I put my arm around her and hugged her tight.

"You have learnt all the words I've prepared. If you don't know a word, just look for me in the crowd. I will give you the answer!" I said hastily. I saw her face brighten up. I wanted to kick myself! Did I just agree to help her CHEAT? THAT WASN'T WHAT I MEANT! But before I could clarify, she dashed off to take her place on stage.

This was the finals of the championship. There were 108 students competing. It took hours before we reached the last round with four contestants still standing. I couldn't have been prouder to see MY BEST FRIEND up there on stage, the ONLY GIRL among the boys! It was sooooo THRILLING! I almost jumped for joy when she got her last word right. It was a really tough one. It was 'tamarind', which refers to a pod-shaped fruit used for its sour juice in cooking. Who would have thought? It was Morticia who picked the word out from her mother's kitchen!

Then, the second last round, one of the three boys was knocked out. He couldn't spell 'balderdash'! My jaw dropped open. Morticia had picked out that word too! It was in her list of 'weird, weird words'! She took over from the boy, and with a huge display of confidence, she spelt the word correctly. WOW, it was down to three people on stage! I jumped up for joy and whooped at her across the ballroom. One of the judges turned to me and raised a warning finger. The announcement over the mike followed next, "Kindly refrain from disrupting the contest!" Oops. I was sooooo happy for her! She's going to make it!

From third position, Morticia moved up to second. Then it was just she and the last boy standing. I hated the look on his face. He was looking at Morticia with a mean sneer. Then her word came, it was 'archaeopteryx'. I froze. A bad feeling rose up my back. It was a dinosaur word, one of those on the list that she had refused to learn because it was hard. I looked towards the stage; just as I had expected, she was searching for me frantically in the crowd. Then she saw me. Her look was one of pure desperation. She pleaded at me with her eyes... I was so TORN! Should I help her? But I didn't want to cheat! But it was the condescending look on the boy's face beside her that made me decide what I should do. I pulled the cockatoo headdress out of my pocket.

My hunch had been right. I'd needed it. I wore it on my head and stood on my chair. I clucked loudly and did a soaring flap of my 'wings'. I turned around on my chair to the thunderous outburst of cheers and claps. People were egging me on! They thought I was playing the fool!

All the judges on stage stood up, FURIOUS! I saw them signal a security guard to get me. I kept on with my dance till I got hauled off the chair. Just before I stepped out of the ballroom, I heard Morticia spell 'archaeopteryx' confidently! She REMEMBERED! It was in the text I sent her after we created the cockatoo dance! I told her to learn the word, 'archaeopteryx', the ancestor of all birds! I'm sooooo proud of her!

I was barred from entering the ballroom after that.
The security guard stood outside the door, glaring at me fiercely. I couldn't care less! I had helped Morticia without cheating. She actually remembered the word!

When the contest was over, people started milling out of the ballroom. I waited anxiously for Morticia. Then I saw her. She looked so TRIUMPHANT with a BIG SMIRK on her face! She saw me and we yelled loudly across the hallway before running into each other's arms. "DID YOU WIN?" I screamed excitedly. People around us smiled and some of the mothers even stopped to pat us on the heads. Morticia said meekly, "I came in second." "WHAT!" I yelled. But my shock turned into a lopsided grin. "I guess that's not bad, well done!" I cried out, genuinely happy for her.

Then a funny thought popped into my head.
"What was the word you couldn't spell?" I asked.

She looked at me and burst out laughing, "I spelt 'c-o-c-k-a-t-u'!" she said, looking really embarrassed. I was stumped. What was that word? Then the champion, the boy who came in first, walked out of the ballroom. He jeered at us, mocking, "Hey GAAALLLs... doing your cockatoo dance now?"

Then it hit me! I couldn't believe Morticia spelt 'COCKATOO' wrong! We looked at each other and started laughing. We laughed and laughed while we slipped into our DANCE! People around us started clapping and encouraging us.

Several people even took a video of us using their handphones. I'm pretty sure we're going to end up even MORE FAMOUS than the obnoxious Spelling Bee Champion!

Just as I had guessed, a YouTube post of our Cockatoo Dance went viral. We were hailed as Singapore's Spelling Bee Cockatoos. I'm proud that I helped my best friend achieve her goal. Although she wasn't crowned Spelling Bee champ, she won something far more valuable. My respect.

I finally found out why Morticia wanted to join the contest so badly, and why she was so afraid that I would compete with her. She wanted to win, to get the prize money for her mother!

I read Morticia's WhatsApp message again. "Mum was pleased that I won second place! I promised to take her for a holiday! It would be her FIRST TIME on a plane!" It felt really good knowing that I had helped to make someone happy. And I'm glad that Morticia can take her mother on a trip! Isn't that sweet?

As for me, next year, it'll be my turn! I deserve nothing less than a shot at winning the Spelling Championship.

CERTIFICATE OF ACKNOWLEDGEMENT

2ND PRIZE

in the Spelling Championship

Awarded to

Morticia Shui

MORTICIA'S CERTIFICATE OF ACKNOWLEDGEMENT

#1 BEST FRIEND IN THE WORLD!

Awarded to

Whoopie Lee

The True Spelling Bee Champ

about the author

Adeline Foo is an MFA graduate of New York University's Tisch School of the Arts, Asia.

She has 20 published children's books, including five national bestsellers. *The Diary of Amos Lee: I Sit, I Write, I Flush!* won the inaugural Red Dot award for 'Best Junior Fiction' presented by the International School Libraries Network (Singapore) in 2009. *The Diary of Amos Lee* is also published in India, Indonesia, China and now, the Slovak Republic. It has also been adapted for a 10-part TV series on Singapore's MediaCorp children's channel, okto.

Adeline is currently developing an inane iPhone game, "Are You A Dodo?" Slated to launch in March 2013, it is zany and obsessive, but the best part? It's a FREE game that all MOTHERS would APPROVE of!

Visit www.amoslee.com.sg for more details.

about the illustrator

Stephanie is a designer at Epigram, a local design house. Epigram started Epigram Books, a publishing arm dedicated to producing well-designed and thought-provoking books (www.epigrambooks.sg).

She is also the illustrator for *The Diary of Amos Lee* series. Stephanie is currently obsessed with her newfound interest, creating GIF animations.

For other adorkable projects and random musings, visit www.steffatplay.blogspot.com.